for Edward

First published in the U.S.A. 1987
by E. P. Dutton,
2 Park Avenue, New York, N.Y. 10016,
a division of NAL Penguin Inc.

Produced by Mathew Price Ltd

Printed in Hong Kong
First American Edition
ISBN: 0-525-44349-5   OBE
10 9 8 7 6 5 4 3 2 1

And so he did.